Haunted House, Haunted Mouse

by JUDY COX

illustrated by
JEFFREY EBBELER

Holiday House / New York

*To all the ghoulies and ghosties and
things that go bump in the night!—J. C.*

For Olivia and Isabel—J. E.

Text copyright © 2011 by Judy Cox
Illustrations copyright © 2011 by Jeffrey Ebbeler
All Rights Reserved
HOLIDAY HOUSE is registered in the U.S. Patent and Trademark Office.
Printed and Bound in March 2012 at Kwong Fat Offset Printing Co., Ltd.,
Dongguan City, China.
The text typeface is Family Dog Fat.
The artwork was created with acrylic paint on paper.
www.holidayhouse.com
3 5 7 9 10 8 6 4

Library of Congress Cataloging-in-Publication Data
Cox, Judy.
Haunted house, haunted mouse / by Judy Cox ; illustrated by Jeffrey Ebbeler. — 1st ed.
p. cm.
Summary: When three costumed trick-or-treaters come to Mouse's door, he crawls
into one of their candy-filled bags to see what Halloween is all about.
ISBN 978-0-8234-2315-6 (hardcover)
[1. Halloween—Fiction. 2. Mice—Fiction.] I. Ebbeler, Jeffrey, ill. II. Title.
PZ7.C83835Hau 2011
[E]—dc22
2010025312

ISBN 978-0-8234-2544-0 (paperback)

One October night the doorbell rang. Mouse peeked out of his hidey-hole. The night was dark; the dark was spooky. On the front porch stood a fearsome trio: a skeleton, a goblin, and a ghost!

But Mouse wasn't scared. His
whiskers twitched as he watched.
    "Trick or treat!" said the skeleton.
    "Trick or treat!" said the goblin.
    "Tick or teak," said a little bitty ghost,
and she tripped over her sheet.
    The three held out their sacks. Dad
plopped one piece of candy in each bag.

"Thank you!" called the kids. The ghost dropped her sack, and goodies spilled out.

Mouse's mouth watered—Yum! He wanted trick-or-treats too. While everyone helped the ghost, Mouse scrambled into the trick-or-treat sack.

Candy! More candy than Mouse had ever seen:
sour balls, gumdrops, lollipops, and chocolate bars.
Mouse closed his eyes and inhaled deeply. His whiskers
wiggled. He simply didn't know where to begin. He
nibbled on this and noshed on that until his cheeks
were as plump as a chipmunk's. Just then the bag
swung high in the air. Where were they going?

Mouse gnawed a peekaboo hole in the paper sack. Dark clouds flitted over the moon. Jack-o'-lanterns sent beams of golden candle-shine flickering across front lawns. Flocks of trick-or-treaters scurried from door to door. Mouse didn't see the candy leaking out, piece by piece, through the peekaboo hole.

The sack swayed like
a pirate ship in a gale.
Mouse's tummy roiled. His
head spun. Poor seasick
Mouse! The next time the
ghost dropped her sack,
Mouse staggered out.

Just then it started to rain. First a drizzle and then a full-out gully washer! The trick-or-treaters dashed for home, holding their coats over their heads.
BOOM! went the thunder.
FLASH! went the lightning.

Away went Mouse. He darted
here and there, dodging raindrops,
splashing through puddles.
Where could he find shelter? He
was lost; he was wet; he was cold.

An abandoned house stood by itself down at the end of the street. The door was barely open, just wide enough for Mouse. Lickety-split—he scampered inside. He didn't notice the sign on the front: KEEP OUT! The door slammed shut behind him. Was that the wind? Or was the house haunted?

Mouse tippawed down the hall to see what he could see. Cobwebs draped over his ears. The house was old; the house was empty. A spooky house filled with creaks and groans and things that went bump in the night.

He heard bones rattle.
A skeleton dancing?
  He saw eyes glimmer.
A goblin prancing?
  A pale shape floated
past. A ghost haunting?

Mouse shook. Mouse shivered. Mouse shuddered. He backed up, step by careful step, until he was against the wall. Trapped!

But Mouse was not afraid. "BOO!" he cried as bold as
a badger. "I'm not afraid of you!"
    Outside the house, the wind blew away the clouds.
Moonlight shone in the windows, revealing . . .

bamboo wind chimes jiggling—
no skeleton.
a green frog croaking—
no goblin.
torn curtains fluttering—
no ghost.

The storm was over. Mouse jumped out the window. He was ready to go home to his safe, dry hidey-hole. But how could he find his way back?

All at once he saw a cherry lollipop shining in the moonlight. He picked it up. Farther down the sidewalk he spied a sour ball. And under the streetlamp, he spotted a scattered row of candy corn. Piece by piece, he followed the candy trail all the way home.

There in his hidey-hole he had a Halloween party of his very own. Good night, spooky night! Happy Trick or Treat!